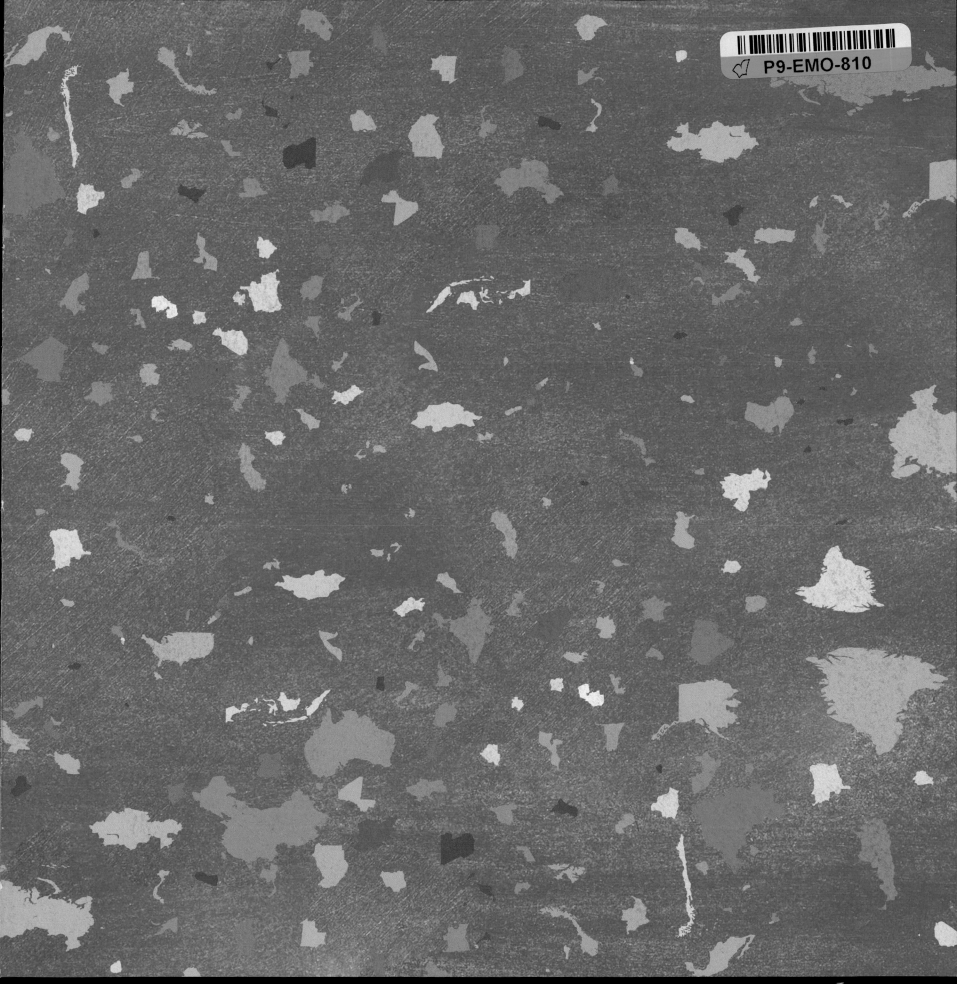

Sweet People

Sweet People Are Everywhere

By *Alice Walker*

Illustrated by *Quim Torres*

T tra.publishing

Are Everywhere

For young Bryon, who is getting a passport

Some of the people in *Turkey*

are very sweet.

Some of those in *Afghanistan*

are very sweet.

Some of the people in the *United States* are very sweet.

In *Canada* too some of the people are sweet.

In *Mexico*

you will definitely find

sweet people.

Likewise in *Sudan.*

There are sweet people among the Zulu in *South Africa* and every language group in *Africa* has some sweet people in it.

There are sweet people in *Iceland*

and in *Russia*.

There are many sweet people in *Korea*.

There are millions of sweet people in *China*.

There are sweet people in *Japan*.

If the sweet people were the leaders

in historically warring countries

they would treat each other

much better!

There are sweet people in *Congo*.

There are sweet people
in *Egypt*

and sweet people
in *Australia.*

Many sweet people are in *Norway*.

Numerous sweet people are in *Spain*.

There are many sweet people in *Ghana*

and *Kenya*

and sweet people also in *Guam*

and the *Philippines*.

There are sweet people in *Cuba*.

Many sweet people exist in *Iran*.

There are sweet people in *Libya*

and *Colombia.*

Sweet people are in *Vietnam.*

Sweet people exist in *England*

and *Myanmar*.

There are

sweet people

for sure

in *Ireland*.

Sweet people are
in *France*.

Sweet people are holding on
in *Syria*.

They are doing the same

in *Iraq.*

Some sweet people live in *Venezuela*.

Many very sweet people live in *Brazil*.

There are sweet people in *Israel*

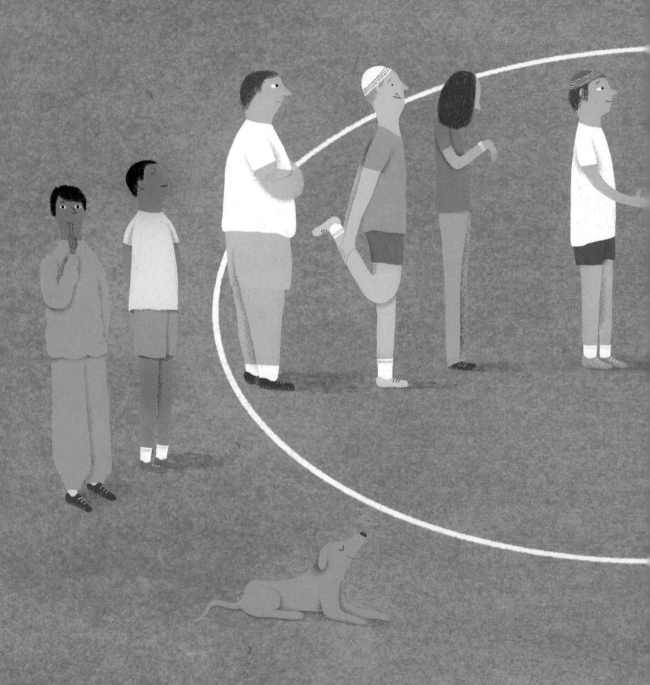

as there are sweet people also in *Palestine.*

Actually, in almost *every house*

on the planet

there is at least one

very sweet person

that you would be happy to know.

Sweet people are *everywhere!*

Being sweet, they must not be disappeared.

We are lost

if we can no longer experience

how sweet human beings can be.

Promise me never

to forget this

no matter

how far

you go

or who sends you.

Iceland
Norway
Canada
England
Ireland
France
United States
Spain
Cuba
Mexico
Venezuela
Ghana
Colombia
Brazil

Russia
Turkey
Syria
Iraq
Afghanistan
China
North Korea
South Korea
Japan
Palestine
Israel
Iran
Libya
Egypt
Myanmar
Vietnam
Sudan
South Sudan
Philippines
Guam
Kenya
Democratic Republic of Congo
Australia

TALKING WITH AUTHOR *Alice Walker*

"I want children reading this to become familiar with the idea that other places exist."

This book is one of dozens of books Alice Walker has written. Her novels, poetry, essays, and children's books have sold more than fifteen million copies, and her writing has been translated into more than two dozen languages. People all over the world read Alice's books! *Sweet People Are Everywhere* is about traveling and meeting people in many different countries, which Alice has done. She likes to travel, but she also likes to be at home in her house in Mendocino, California, which is way out in the country. When we spoke to her, she was sitting on her deck and looking out at the mountains. She told us she loves living in the country. She is thankful that she grew up in the countryside, in Putnam County, Georgia, where she was born in 1944. Her parents were farmers and she was the youngest of eight children. Because she was the youngest, she was called Baby Alice. And when she was very small—still just a baby—she started writing. And she has not stopped!

The words of this book are a poem you wrote that is dedicated to "young Bryon, who is getting a passport." Who is young Bryon?
Young Bryon was a houseguest of mine. He was a teenage musician planning a trip to China. Though he was nineteen or so, he had never traveled outside of the United States. He was nervous about being so far from his home and his church, where he played gospel music on piano.

What did you say to help him feel less nervous?
I encouraged him to think of the whole experience as an adventure. I wanted to assure him that no matter what a country's government is doing while you are visiting, the people continue to be like people everywhere. They are caring for their children, their gardens, their fields, or learning new amazements on their computers. The Bryon in this poem wants to see the world, and he needs to see the world. He is going to meet other people who are like him. I wanted him to feel like the world is small, really. The poem was written to him and sparked by his adventure, but it is for all young people.

There are thirty-seven different places that you write about in this book. Places like Ireland and Iraq, Venezuela and Vietnam, Kenya and Korea. Have you been to the countries you mention here?

I have been to some of them. I came from a tiny place in Georgia, and I had no idea there were people all around the world. They told me if I dug deep enough, I would reach China. But really, I had no idea. I want children reading this to become familiar with the idea that other places exist.

Do you like to travel?

Every chance I have had to go and see someplace, I have taken it! And that is how I discovered the sameness in people. You can kind of recognize yourself in everyone. *Gulliver's Travels* is not really the truth. I mean, there is truth in it, but you don't go to a city and people are horses. They are you and your parents, but they may be a different color and wearing different clothing. There are not "foreign" countries. You get over there and yes, the food is different but you love it. And the people are the same.

When did you start writing?

Shortly after birth. My mother says that when I was crawling, I was writing in the dirt with a stick. I was writing poetry by the time I was nine. But I was memorizing it and reciting it much earlier.

What drew you to poetry at such a young age?

My family had the book *Prose and Poetry*, and my older sister who was in college would read it to us when she came home. And I could see it. The fascination of seeing what someone else is reading is extraordinary.

When did you decide you wanted to write stories and poems of your own?

Someone gave me *Gulliver's Travels* just before I turned twelve. The wonder of that book! I was someone who had never thought about those creatures—creatures like tiny people and giants and horses that talk. Part of my impetus for writing was wanting to help others see what I was feeling.

What do you like the most about writing?

It's magic. You can create something. And you can make it so visual that other people can see it, but it actually comes out of the invisible.

Besides being a writer, you are also an activist. What kind of causes do you work for?

So many causes! My deepest concern is for the children of the world. Right up there with the animals of the planet. And on and on. There is a whole long list! It is not just that nature is being destroyed. Children all over the world are being harmed.

What would you do if you were not a writer?

I wanted to be a scientist at one point. And a pianist at another. And those things were completely unaffordable. I don't regret anything. When doors are closed that you wanted to open as a child, you realize that perhaps part of your reason for being is to open them for others. And that is part of what this poem is about.

Do you have advice for children who want to explore their creativity?

Yes! In order to create art, you have to have tools. Paper and crayons and maybe paint. If you are really small, ask your parents for supplies. You don't have to write in the dirt with a twig like I did. But I love that image because it shows that even as an infant, I knew I had to have a tool. I wasn't using my fingers—I was using twigs. If you have the desire to make something, you are making it virtually out of nothing. Think about what you need to do that and acquire those things.

Is there anything you would like to say to the children reading this book?

I would like to tell them to go with their spirit. If we could just help kids get away from television and all of the gadgets more, they would have more time to create and to be present in themselves.

NOTES ON THE ILLUSTRATIONS

Who is Bryon?
This book is dedicated to Young Bryon. To learn who he is, read the interview with author Alice Walker.

Mexico:
The two girls running are members of the Tarahumara, or Rarámuri (meaning "those who run fast") tribe, who live in the Copper Canyon region of northwestern Mexico and are legendary for their ability to run very long distances. Rarájipari is the name of a traditional running game they play, in which the women use sticks and hoops and the men kick a wooden ball.

Iceland:
In the background of this image are the northern lights, which are beautiful curtains of colored lights. They are most visible late at night in northern parts of the world, such as Iceland, during the winter and spring. The northern lights occur because the solar wind (from the sun) blows out electrons that glow when they mix with gases in the Earth's atmosphere.

Russia:
In this illustration, it is the middle of winter in Russia. In a clearing in the forest, a grandfather and granddaughter are playing chess. In Russia, people play chess outdoors in the winter, even when it is snowing!

Korea, China, and Japan:
These are all countries in Asia. Bicycles are widely used in all three of these countries; often people commute to work by bike. The tree in Japan is a flowering cherry tree. Japan is famous all over the world for its cherry blossoms (called sakura) and people have parties (called hanami) under the trees to celebrate these beautiful flowers.

Congo:
In Congo, families and friends often gather under trees just like this one to spend time together talking, drinking tea, and playing games.

Ghana, Kenya, Guam, Philippines:
Kids all over the world love to play games. In Ghana, these kids are playing the Great Snake—the children holding hands are the snake and they try to catch others. In Kenya, this game with marbles is called bano (the word means marbles in Swahili). Chongka is the game with the wooden board that they are playing in Guam. Luksong Tinik is what these kids in the Philippines are playing—the words mean "jumping over thorns" and to play it, the jumper leaps over the kids sitting on the ground.

Cuba and Iran:
The musical instruments in these two pictures are special to these countries, and they are also a tribute to Bryon, the person to whom the book is dedicated, since he is a musician.

Myanmar:
The man in a red robe walking on the sidewalk is a Buddhist monk. Buddhism is a religion, and Myanmar is considered the most religious Buddhist country in the world. Ninety percent of the country's population is Buddhist. The letters on the yellow building are the words for food store in Burmese, the official language of Myanmar.

Syria and Iraq:
You will see birds in both of these pictures. These birds are doves, which are traditionally symbols of peace and love.

Venezuela and Brazil:
Both scenes here show poor areas of these countries—in Venezuela these areas are called barrios and in Brazil they are called favelas. The kites are symbols of hope and freedom. Kids everywhere fly kites—sometimes they even make their own kites out of material such as paper or plastic bags.

Israel and Palestine:
Soccer games between Israeli and Palestinian children are often organized by various groups that bring these kids together so they can get to know each other. This illustration imagines a day when girls and boys and religious and secular children come together in play and friendship.

Map:
This map shows each of the countries mentioned in *Sweet People Are Everywhere.*

AUTHOR
Alice Walker

ILLUSTRATOR
Quim Torres

PUBLISHER & CREATIVE DIRECTOR
Ilona Oppenheim

ART DIRECTOR & DESIGNER
Jefferson Quintana
ILONA Creative Studio

EDITOR
Andrea Gollin

WRITING CREDITS
Interview with Alice Walker: *Andrea Gollin*

PRINTING
Printed and bound in China by
Shenzhen Reliance Printers

First printing June 2021

COVER

Illustration: *Quim Torres*

Cover design: *Jefferson Quintana*

MIX
Paper from
responsible sources
FSC® C102842

Tra Publishing is committed to sustainability
in its materials and practices.

Tra Publishing
245 NE 37th Street
Miami, FL 33137
trapublishing.com

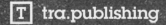